I.D.

They see the things we can't see....

WATCHERS

WATCHERS

I.D.

PETER LERANGIS

AN
APPLE
PAPERBACK

SCHOLASTIC INC.
New York Toronto London Auckland Sydney
Mexico City New Delhi Hong Kong

No part of this publication may be reproduced in whole or in part, or stored in a retrieval system, or transmitted in any form or by any means, electronic, mechanical, photocopying, recording, or otherwise, without written permission of the publisher. For information regarding permission, write to Scholastic Inc., Attention: Permissions Department, 555 Broadway, New York, NY 10012.

ISBN 0-590-10998-7

12 11 10 9 8 7 6 5 4 3 2 1   9/9 0 1 2 3 4/0

Printed in the U.S.A.   40
First Scholastic printing, January 1999

I.D.

WATCHERS
Case File: 1449

Name: Baby 5

Age: 0

First contact: 40.08.19

Acceptance:

1

She is born.
She breathes.
She feels.
She shrieks.
At the cold. The light. The pain.
No retreat now. No comfort.
Just instinct.
A pair of hands lifts her. Wraps her in a blanket.
"We did it," whispers a deep voice. "Again."
She turns to the sound. Tries to focus on a face.

A door opens.

She moves. Sheltered by the arms.

Warm.

Her screams fade to whimpers.

She goes limp.

She sleeps.

When she awakens, the arms are carrying her through a shaft of blazing white.

"Did the mother leave a note?" *asks a voice. Different. Softer. Higher.*

"No." *The deep one. The one that makes her rumble.*

"Look at the resemblance. It must be the same mother."

"Have you notified the ICU, Dr. Rudin?"

"Of course."

"Would you get the paperwork started for the adoption process?"

"Same agency as the last?"

"Please hurry. I need your help."

"What shall I tell your daughter?"

"Tell her I'll be another couple of hours." *Words. Rhythms. Gentle. Yes.* "Please have somebody order her dinner."

Motion. Speed. Sleep.

* * *

4

Before leaving Dr. Black, Julia Rudin adjusts the sleeping infant's head. Briskly but delicately. In midstride.

On the back of the baby's neck she spots a red arrow-shaped birthmark. The same as the other foundling — how long ago? A year?

As Dr. Black barges through the ICU door, the child's face is peaceful. Trusting.

Dr. Rudin turns away and walks to a small waiting room. There, a twelve-year-old girl reads a magazine.

"Sorry, Whitney," the young doctor begins. "Sort of bad news. Your dad told me — "

The girl puts down the magazine and looks up. "Eve," she says.

"What?"

"That's the baby's name. Eve."

"How do you know?"

Whitney smiles. And shrugs.

As the girl turns to pick up the magazine again, Dr. Rudin notices something on her neck.

A mark. Red and arrow-shaped.

What is he doing?

He has a plan. If it works, he's a genius.

If it doesn't?

He's a murderer.

2

"**W**ould you come into the den, dear?"
Eve stopped eating.
She knew.
She knew from Mommy's tone of voice.
Nice.
And worried.
Nice and worried was a bad combination.
But why? Why now?
Because I need to know sometime, Eve
thought.

Mommy and Daddy had never told her the
truth about where she came from; they didn't

want to admit it, but *Eve* knew, oh, yes she did, it was OBVIOUS, because she didn't *look* like them — not in person, not in pictures, not the slightest bit — and just because she was only six years old didn't mean she was *stupid* or anything.

"Eve, darling? Did you hear me?" her mom called again.

Eve tried to answer, but no sound came out.

I can't go in there.

But she had to.

Somebody had to. Or Mommy would get mad.

Eve closed her eyes. She reached into her brain. She could be someone else.

Caroline.

[Yes. That's me.]

Caroline wasn't afraid. She had a great big room and her parents weren't allowed in. She was smart and strong and *nothing* bothered her.

[I don't have to go inside until I want to!]

Eve looked up from the kitchen table. "Wait a minute! I'm eating!"

Did Mommy and Daddy yell? No sir, not at Caroline — and *you bet* they would have yelled at plain old Eve.

Caroline was *so* cool.

Eve took her time finishing. And then cleared her plate. And then found her yo-yo.

And *then* went inside.

"Yeah?"

Mommy was sitting on the sofa, Daddy in the armchair. But the TV wasn't on and they were leaning forward. Smiling.

Sad-smiling.

"Have a seat, dear."

Think. Say something. Do something.

[Just sit.]

Eve tossed back her hair and sat on the sofa.

"Sweetie . . . um, remember when your teacher asked everyone in the class to bring in old baby pictures?" Mommy asked.

"And you wanted to know why we didn't have any photos from the hospital?" Daddy added.

"Or photos of Mommy pregnant?" Mommy said.

Here it comes I hate this no no no NO . . .

[Yeah. So?]

"I'm sure you've been . . . well, expecting this — " Mommy said.

"*Sus*pecting," Daddy corrected gently.

"Right. The truth is, Eve, Mommy never *was* pregnant, because . . ."

Crying. Mommy was beginning to cry.

I can't hear the words I CAN'T . . .

And when Mommy finally said it, when the truth came out exactly the way Eve always thought it would (the *A* word, the *A* word), Caroline was history. She faded away, leaving Eve all alone. And Eve was falling, falling into a hole that had no bottom.

"We know how you must feel," Daddy was saying.

"We love you just the same," Mommy added. "This doesn't change anything."

Yes it does, it changes EVERYTHING.

She wasn't theirs.

An *agency*. They got her from an *agency*.

Somebody you paid money to.

NO NO NO NO NO NO NO NO NO . . .

Eve stood up from the sofa. She turned and walked to the bookshelf.

"Eve?" Mommy said.

NOT EVE. I CAN'T BE EVE. And not Caroline, because she ran away.

12

Alexis.

Yes. That's who she'd be.

Alexis wouldn't stand for this. She'd be mad. REAL mad.

[I hate them. I hate their house. HOW COULD THEY DO THIS TO ME?]

Eve wrapped her hand around a vase and pulled. With a loud smash, it hit the floor and broke into a million pieces.

Daddy leaped off his chair, but Mommy held him back.

Eve began yanking Mommy's college books from the shelf. They made a cool swishy noise when they hit the floor with the pages open. Eve burst out laughing.

[WHEEEEEEEEE!]

She ran into the living room. Mommy's African violets looked so soft and perfect, all bright in the sunlight. She grabbed one of them and crushed it. Then another. The next one came out by the roots.

"Eve, stop that!" Mommy called out.

[You're not my mommy, are you? I can do whatever I want!]

Daddy was picking up the pieces of broken pottery, on his knees, looking like he wanted to be angry but had forgotten how. "Oh, Eve," he said.

Stop stop stop what am I doing?

And just like that, Alexis was gone, and Eve was tumbling again, falling hard.

So she thought of Danielle.

Danielle found the whole thing *so ridiculous.* Daddy on his knees, the purple flowers all crumpled like wilted lettuce.

She began to laugh. She sat on the living room sofa, doubling over.

But the moment she hit the cushions, Mommy sat next to her. And the laughing stopped.

Mommy's eyes were wide and brimming with tears.

Danielle shouldn't laugh. She was being so bad.

So who? Who?

Eve reached again.

Maybe Bryann. Sad, delicate Bryann.

Eve could feel the pressure welling up in her eyes.

Then Mommy leaned toward her. And hugged her. And the arms felt the same as always. Big and warm and just right. Like a mother's.

When the tears came, they weren't Bry-ann's. Or anyone else's.

They were Eve's.

And she thought they'd never end.

New report.

Go ahead.

W. G., of Bloomington, Indiana. Alzheimer's.

Age fourteen?

Yes.

Like the others.

3

"This is the Beast?" Kate Cranston gazed down the slope. "I'd call this, like, early *intermediate*."

Eve stopped. She kept her skis pointed along the beginner trail, which crossed the Beast and wound gently through a wide wooded path.

Eve was a much better skier than Kate. Even though she was only in eighth grade, not quite fourteen yet, she practiced with the high school team and could beat some of the ninth- and tenth-graders.

The Beast *wasn't* a super-hard trail. But on a day like this, when the trail disappeared into the whiteness of a gathering snowstorm, and the lodge was visible only as a faint cluster of lights below, slower was better.

"Uh, Kate? I need *both* my legs," Eve said. "I'm hoping for another ski trip or two this winter."

Kate didn't take the hint. "Race you."

"Kate, stop it — "

"Afraid you'll lose?"

"*No way*, but — "

"I'll go by myself."

Eve *hated* these conversations. But Kate was Kate. She *would* go down alone. And if anything happened to her, Eve would feel responsible.

Eve began turning downhill. "You know, this is a dumb idea."

"On your mark . . ." Kate replied. "Get set . . ."

She shoved off. "*Byyyyyyyye!*"

"*Hey!*" Eve protested.

She jigged her skis into place. Crouched.

Knees together. Body forward, over the skis. PUSH — left . . . right . . . left . . .

Eve gained ground fast. Kate's movements were wild, jerky.

"WOOOOOOO!" Eve screamed.

Kate screamed back.

The whipping snow felt like sand against Eve's face. Below her, the lodge was materializing out of the whiteness. Looming up fast.

She didn't see the other girl coming.

Just a flash of red and yellow.

Then a crash.

Eve's shoulders lurched sideways. Her knees twisted. She hit the slope, sending up a spray of white. Her cheeks scraped the icy surface as her skis flew off.

She stopped sliding a few yards east of the lift line.

The other girl was lying toe to toe with Eve, on her back.

Eve scrambled to her feet. No broken bones. That was a relief.

Kate skied to a stop beside them. "What was *that*?"

Eve was standing over the stranger. The girl wasn't moving. Her skin was flushed, her eyes fluttering.

"Are you okay?" Eve asked.

"Uh-huh," the girl replied.

"She doesn't look okay," Kate murmured. "I'll get some help."

As Kate skied back toward the lodge, Eve knelt over the girl and felt her forehead. Red-hot.

The girl grimaced and tried to sit up.

"You have a fever," Eve said. "Just stay still and wait for the ski patrol."

"I can't breathe." The girl was pulling at her down coat now, trying to yank it open.

Eve cradled the girl's head in her lap. She helped her with the zipper. "I'm Eve."

"Tanya," the girl said. "Where's my mom?"

"I'm sure she's coming. Sit tight. You'll be okay."

Eve looked over her shoulder. Three ski patrollers were speeding toward them, pulling a sled.

"I'm — I can't — " Tanya's eyes flickered shut. Her breaths were shallow and erratic. The redness was purpling.

She's passing out.

"Breathe!" Eve urged. "Hang on, they're coming!"

Tanya nodded vaguely. Her eyes opened, frightened and pleading. "Help me."

Arms. Pushing.

Eve lost her balance. She scrambled to her feet.

Three burly ski patrollers were kneeling around Tanya.

They asked her a few questions, then gently eased her onto the sled. One of them began to shout into a walkie-talkie.

As they pulled her away, a crowd formed around Eve. A bright sea of Gore-Tex and nylon. In the distance, she spotted an ambulance swerving into the parking lot to meet the sled.

She tried to elbow her way forward.

"Eve, are you all right?" Mom's voice.

"Yes!" Eve shouted. Tanya was vanishing, swallowed up by the gawkers.

"What did you do to her?" That was Kate.

"It wasn't me!" Eve said.

She could hear mutterings: "food poisoning" . . . "broken leg" . . . "hotdogging."

No. Something worse.

As the ambulance sped away, siren blaring, Eve began to shiver uncontrollably. The wind seared through her coat.

Mom and Dad were on either side of her now.

"Sh-she skied r-right into me," Eve explained. "S-s-something's wrong with her."

"Let's go inside, honey," Dad said, putting his arm around her.

There. Tanya's family.

A mom, dad, son. The resemblance was unmistakable. They were being escorted by a ski official toward a station wagon.

"Excuse me?" she called out, jogging after them. "Wait!"

The man helped the family into the backseat and shut the door. He shot Eve an impatient look.

"I was the girl Tanya collided with," Eve said. "Where did they take her?"

"Keene Mountain Hospital," the man replied, climbing into the driver's side.

"Is she going to be okay?" Eve pressed on.

The window rolled open. "Too early to tell," the man said.

"What happened to her?"

The car's engine roared to life, but not enough to obscure the answer.

"Heart attack."

Bernsen. Second case this week.

The girl with her is Case 1449.

So there's hope.

But she doesn't know.

How old is she?

By their measurements, thirteen years, eleven months, and two weeks.

She'd better find out soon.

4

"No history of heart trouble on either side of the family, Mr. and Mrs. Bernsen?"

"No."

"Has Tanya been taking any new medication?"

"No."

"Any signs of illness, weakness, shortness of breath?"

"Well, yes. But she has occasional asthma. She insisted she'd be all right skiing. . . ."

Eve could hear the voices all the way in the waiting room. They floated in from an examining area down the hall. She hated listening. Tanya's parents sounded so wounded and confused, the doctor so cold and clinical.

She tried to ignore them.

Sit tight. Give it a few minutes.

Someone would be out soon. A doctor who knew about cases like this, who'd tell them that Tanya was going to be just fine.

Kate was sitting to Eve's left, eyes fixed on a TV that droned overhead. Mr. and Mrs. Hardy sat to Eve's right, reading magazines. Around them, patients walked in and out, some on crutches, almost all wearing plaster casts — sprains, broken bones, injuries you were *supposed* to get at a ski resort.

Not a heart attack.

The eyes.

Eve couldn't stop thinking about Tanya's eyes. The way they'd looked *at* and *through* Eve at the same time. The way they'd seemed to focus on something just behind her. Something dark and horribly unexpected, but somehow inevitable.

Just once had Eve ever seen anything like it — a year earlier, the only time she'd been hunting with her dad. They'd just about given up when they'd spotted a deer within range. The moment Mr. Hardy had taken aim, it turned toward them. Its eyes had instantly flashed with the knowledge that it was going to die. But rather than run, it had leveled its gaze at Eve. Not in fear, exactly, or even panic. Something more like accusation. As if to say, *Not now. Not like this. Not fair.*

Eve had screamed. Her dad's shot had gone wild, and the deer had fled. Even so, Eve thought about those eyes for weeks.

Now she'd seen them again. Closer.

But human. And much more terrifying.

Tanya was her age. Fourteen-year-old kids didn't get heart attacks.

Things like this happen, and there's no explanation.

Eve had to see her again. She had to see what Tanya really looked like. Without the death stare. With hope. With something like a normal, everyday *kid* expression.

It seemed like hours before Tanya's parents finally returned to the waiting room.

"She's out of Intensive Care," Mrs. Bernsen said. "Serious condition."

"Meaning better than critical," her husband explained. "But worse than stable. We'll know more tomorrow."

Tomorrow?

They'd all be home by then.

"Well, best of luck," Eve's dad said, standing up.

"We'll call," her mom added.

After a grim farewell, Eve left with her parents and Kate. A light snow was falling as they walked into the parking lot.

"A teenage kid with a heart attack?" Kate murmured. "It's bizarre, Eve. It's *unnatural*. Especially with no family history."

"Stuff like that can skip generations," Eve suggested. "Maybe she got it from, like, a great-grandparent."

Kate shook her head. "Dream on."

"What do *you* think it is?"

"I think it's something big, Eve. Like an epidemic."

"It's a *heart attack*. You don't get a heart attack from germs!"

"What if it's something that makes the body *get* a heart attack?"

"Oh, please." Eve reached the car and opened the back door.

"Five years ago a kid in California dies of hardening of the arteries," Kate said, climbing in after Eve. "A couple of years later, a girl in Ohio loses her hair and develops osteoporosis. That's weakening of the bones. An old-people's disease."

"Where do you *get* this stuff?" Eve asked.

"I surf, therefore I am," Kate replied. "It's been on a lot of the news sites. I couldn't believe the first case, so I kept looking."

"The storm is breaking up," Mr. Hardy remarked as he pulled out of the lot. "I say we head home now, while it's still daylight."

"Shouldn't we eat first?" Mrs. Hardy asked.

"We can eat on the road," Mr. Hardy suggested.

"Another girl's teeth fall out," Kate barreled on, "and she develops chronic constipation — "

"*Kate!*" Mrs. Hardy exclaimed.

"I *was* hungry, up until a minute ago," Eve grumbled.

"All I can say is, there's more to this

than meets the eye," Kate said, folding her arms.

Eve threw herself into frantic packing. The weekend was over. Time to move on. Time to stop thinking about

The eyes.

They were following her still. Telling her something. Still looking over her shoulder.

"Dad," she said as they loaded the luggage into the car, "can we stop by the hospital?"

He smiled impatiently. "It's only been an hour and a half. We'll call from the road, okay?"

Eve and Kate settled into the backseat. Mr. and Mrs. Hardy sat up front.

As the car pulled away, snow crunched dully under the tires. Mrs. Hardy turned on the radio and surfed for a weather report.

Eve settled back. She tried to block the memory, but the image kept returning *(the eyes)*.

Soon Tanya would be all right, and the eyes would disappear.

Stop thinking.

She tried to focus on the radio. Listen. Block out all memories.

The stations blipped in and out. A Top 40 song. Static. A scratchy classical piece. A foreign-language broadcast. More static.

" . . . at a loss to speculate on the latest development at Keene Mountain Hospital . . ." a voice intoned.

Eve sat up. *"Leave it there!"*

" . . . where tonight a fourteen-year-old, Tanya Bernsen," the voice continued, "after a heroic attempt to save her life by a team of specialists, has died. . . ."

Tally of deceased has risen to seventy-three.

Pending?

At least a dozen others. Very few are related. The mutation is occurring at random.

The strain is stronger than we thought.

5

The words "LEBANON VALLEY GAZETTE OBITUARIES" flashed across Kate's computer screen.

" 'Sarah Fischer, fourteen,' " Eve read, " 'of complications from gout.' "

"See?" Kate said. "Who gets gout at our age? *Nobody!*"

Eve began clicking furiously, opening Kate's bookmarks. Names and faces blinked on and off. More deaths: Meryl Haber, Walter Gilbert, Bryann Davis, Francine Etkowitz . . .

"This is sick, Kate."

"I *know*. Scroll to the bottom. One of the names has a link."

" 'Alexis Wainwright . . . several days before her fourteenth birthday' . . . blah blah blah . . . 'premature hardening of the arteries' . . . 'for more information, click on . . .' Bingo."

Eve clicked. Another site assembled itself on the screen:

JOURNAL OF THE SOCIETY OF GENETICS AND PATHOLOGY

Premature Telomere Foreshortening in Chromosome of Adolescent

Speculation over the role of telomere length in the aging process took a leap forward in the death of a teenage girl in Cold Harbor, whose aberrant genetic makeup was seen as a primary cause of preternatural senescence. Further investigation revealed the existence of the damaged chromosome in one of the parents, who remains asymptomatic.

"You're the science genius," Kate said. "Do you understand this *at all*?"

"I think I do," Eve replied. "You have these things in your body — chromosomes. You get them from your parents. They contain DNA, which make the genes, which build the proteins that make you *you*. Sixth-grade biology, right?"

"I must have been absent that day."

"Anyway, the chromosomes have these wavy things at the ends, like tails. They're called telomeres. Ours are, like, totally buff, because we're young. But once you hit our parents' age, forget it. The telomeres shrink. Some scientists think that telomeres control aging. They give the body instructions on how to get old — you know, they tell the skin to sag, the hair to fall out . . ."

"That is so disgusting."

"Anyway, this girl's telomeres shrank too early," Eve explained.

"Duh."

"She inherited this mutated gene from one of her parents, who didn't actually have the disease. Her mom or dad just carried the gene, then passed it on to her."

"So this girl died of *old age*."

"Or some part of her body aged too quickly."

"Like I said. Same thing with Tanya's heart. Same thing with the other kids. See? I'm not as dumb as I look. It's an epidemic!"

"It's a *theory*, Kate," Eve cautioned. "Read the first word of the article. 'Speculation.' They don't know."

"All great discoveries start this way." Kate grabbed the mouse. "We are on the verge of something big, Eve. A Tony Award."

"Nobel Prize."

"Whatever. We'll split the proceeds. I think I can find some other sites, too."

As Kate began surfing, images flickered on the screen. Photos. Icons. Text.

A face.

It had flashed briefly. Not long enough to get a good look.

"Wait!" Eve said.

"What?" Kate asked.

"Go back."

Kate clicked once, twice . . .

Blink.

The face again. A yearbook photo. Staring off into the distance. Like a million other poses of a million other junior high school kids.

It was captioned ALEXIS WAINWRIGHT.

But the face was familiar.

My face.

40

No. The hair was different. Shorter. And Eve would never have worn a ripped T-shirt in a formal photo.

Eve knelt. Looked into the eyes.

The eyes.

I know them.

Mine.

But not mine.

"Weird." Kate's finger was frozen over the mouse. "She looks exactly like you."

She's a stranger.

That's all.

A photo of a face.

She probably looks nothing like you in person.

Looked *like you. She's dead.*

"Eve? Earth to Eve!"

Eve's eyes were glued to the name now.

It brought something to mind. An image.

A girl from her past.

The strong one.

The angry one.

The eyes stared at her. *It's me*, they were saying. *Me, Alexis.*

NO!

This is ridiculous.

A coincidence.

No. Big. Deal.

"Eve?" Kate repeated. "You're scaring me."

Eve took a deep breath. "Sorry. I was thinking about when I was little — when I was upset. I'd become this bratty kid, and her name was — "

"Alexis!" Kate blurted out.

"You remember?"

"Do I? You were, like, *possessed."*

"Well, so, you know — the face, the name. It kind of freaked me out."

Kate fell silent. She was staring at the screen now. "Oh, my god."

"What?"

"Why did you pick that name — Alexis?"

Eve shrugged. "It sounded cool, I guess."

"You didn't know *anyone* by that name?"

"Nope."

"Not even from your deepest past? From before you were adopted?"

"I was a newborn! How could I?"

"We don't *forget* our early memories, Eve. Even I know that. You *had* to have seen your birth mother, right? Maybe your birth father, too. You heard their voices."

"Okay. So?"

"So, what if the couple had an older daughter? What if her name was Alexis?"

Sister.

Parents.

"Wait," Eve said. "You think — this girl is my — "

Leave.

Now.

Don't listen.

"*Look* at her, Eve."

"Kate, that is so totally — "

Look.

The eyes.

I know them.

NO.

How could I?

A face. A name. That's all. Chance.

"What?" Kate said. "What is it? Am I right? Are you remembering?"

She's putting ideas in your head.

Go. Quick.

"Uh, Kate, I don't like this — "

"You have to find them, Eve!"

"Who?"

"Your birth parents. The Wainwrights!"

43

"They're not my birth parents!"

"Eve, it's so obvious."

"There are millions of faces, Kate. On millions of Web sites. And this one just happens to be my long-lost sister? From my long-lost family? *Does that make sense to you?"*

"Okay, I know you don't *want* to believe it. I don't blame you. Sometimes the truth is hard — "

"I know the truth already!"

You HAVE parents.

You are Eve Hardy. Not Eve Wainwright.

Eve bolted. Opened the door.

"But what if I'm right?"

Kate's words stopped Eve cold.

What if?

Mom. Dad. For real.

A sister, too. And me.

A family.

Happy.

Once upon a time.

Eve sank against the doorjamb. "Kate, you don't understand what you're doing to me."

"You have to know," Kate said gently. "Knowledge is power. *You* once told me that."

"What if they *are* my birth family? They

didn't raise me. They weren't there for me. Why should I care about them? Why should I cross the country for them? So they can throw me out again? Or so they can fall on their knees and apologize? Either way, what do I get?"

"A family medical history," Kate replied.

"A *what*?"

"Alexis died because of the disease, Eve. The disease could be genetic. You're her sister!"

It makes no sense.

I CAN'T BE HER SISTER.

I CAN'T HAVE THE —

THE —

The eyes.

Again.

Following her.

Beckoning.

From the screen.

From the dead.

With a click, they would disappear from the screen.

But they would never leave Eve's mind.

They know.

They live.

In me.

Nothing made sense.

But it didn't have to.

Some things never did.

Eve stood frozen, indecisive, her hand on the doorknob.

Then, slowly, she shut the door. "Ski camp is coming up. We'll be away from home for two weeks."

"I can cover for you," Kate said quietly. "Your parents don't have to know where you really are."

"Can your brother help us?"

"We'll say he's driving us to camp. He can drop you off at the train station."

"I couldn't lie. I'd have to write Mom and Dad and let them know."

"Suit yourself."

Eve scowled. "I just don't know . . ."

"Don't you?"

Eve thought about it. But this was beyond thought. Beyond reason.

This was instinct.

"I hope Cold Harbor isn't too far away," she said with a sigh.

Kate smiled.

Does this one have a chance?

As much as the ones who came
before her. No more.

6

"*F*rrrrreeport next!*"

The conductor's voice woke Eve from a deep sleep.

Her cheek was pressed against fabric. Wool.

A sweater. A stranger's.

"Oh!" Eve jerked away, red-faced.

The elderly lady next to her smiled and dusted off her shoulder. "It's okay, I didn't have the heart to move," she said sweetly. "They're very lucky, your mom and dad."

"They are?"

"You talked about them. In your sleep."

"I did?"

The old lady chuckled. "I know quite a bit about you, Alexis."

Alexis.

The Wainwright house.

Red brick. Big lawn. Lamppost with a swinging wooden sign.

I'm playing on the front lawn. Digging holes. Burying Ken because he dissed Barbie.

Dad is turning up the driveway in his car. He's angry.

Not Dad.

Mr. Wainwright.

Eve shivered.

Stop.

It was a dream.

I am NOT Alexis.

She tried to focus. Her dreams were wild. Confusing.

Flashes from her childhood.

When she used to think she *was* Alexis.

The fantasy Alexis. Not the possible-sister Alexis.

She couldn't *be* her sister. That didn't make sense.

Eve looked at the faces of the boarding passengers, the strangers she'd never seen and would never see again.

That's what the Wainwrights are. Strangers.

I am barging in on strangers.

She began to shake. The whole idea seemed ridiculous.

Sneaking away. Lying.

Showing up at someone's house unannounced. Without even the courtesy of a phone call.

I did call them.

Okay, I hung up as soon as I heard Mrs. Wainwright's voice.

But I had to.

They wouldn't have believed me.

Or they would have freaked.

I couldn't have handled any of that.

I would have chickened out. The whole trip would have fallen apart.

I have to see with my own eyes. This is the only way to do it.

The train was beginning to move again.

Cold Harbor was the next stop.

She looked out the window.

Calm. Down.

Outside was an undulating countryside dotted with stone houses. A distant line of cross-country skiers glided along a ridge, and the smell of burning firewood permeated even the closed train car.

It was gorgeous. Perfect.

This is where I would have lived if —

Stop.

She couldn't think of that.

But they're rich if they live here. Rich people don't give up their children.

Maybe I was awful. Unbearable.

She glanced at her ticket. Round trip. Good any time.

Stay on the platform. Catch the next train back.

Don't go. Don't remind them. Don't find out what you could have been but never will be —

Soon the train began to slow. The loudspeaker crackled.

"CO-O-O-O-OLD HARBOR!" the conductor announced.

A station pulled into view. It was decked with holiday lights. Fresh-fallen snow coated the slate roof and gingerbread latticework. A small crowd of people dressed in winter coats gazed up hopefully at the train, their arms laden with gifts.

Stay.

Go.

Eve stood.

She grabbed her backpack from the overhead rack. Saying good-bye to the old lady, she numbly stepped into the aisle.

As she walked toward the door, she rubbed the back of her neck.

For some reason, it was throbbing.

Right where her birthmark was.

It has begun.

1

Four seventy-seven.

Eve paused in front of the white-shingled house.

Forest-green shutters. A lamppost marked WAINWRIGHT, swinging in the wind. A cobble-stone walkway, freshly snow-blown. Chimes on the front porch.

Perfect.

Cozy. Homey. A place she could have been happy growing up in.

To the right, tire tracks led up the driveway toward a closed two-car garage.

Somebody was home.

Snap.

A light. Through the left bay window. A dining room. A woman sitting at the table. Bathed in warm amber light.

Eve's breath shuddered.

This is crazy.

What are you going to say to her?

Eve turned away.

"Can I help you?"

A car was gliding to a stop in the driveway. The driver, a man wearing a fur hat, was looking at her curiously through his open window.

"Huh?" Eve squeaked.

"Are you looking for somebody?"

The face was friendly. Open. Matter-of-fact. Kind.

Familiar.

Now or never.

Eve's hand reached up to the brim of her floppy hat. She slowly took it off and looked him in the eye.

"Mr. Wainwright?" she said softly.

His face went slack.

The engine stopped. The man was opening the door now. Stepping out.

Eve backed away.

Mr. Wainwright stopped in his tracks. "Sorry," he said, averting his eyes embarrassedly. "I — I don't mean to stare — it's just that you look . . ."

Eve swallowed hard. "Like Alexis?"

When the man glanced up at her again, his face was hollow, fearful. *"Who are you?"*

"Eve Hardy. I think."

"How do you know Alexis?"

"I'm not s-sure."

Eve shivered. Her jaw was numb. She could barely feel her toes or fingers.

Mr. Wainwright gestured toward the front door. "Please, come in."

As they approached, the door opened. The woman inside was smiling. "Hi, honey. How was — "

The words died in her mouth. Her face went pale.

Mr. Wainwright took his wife's arm. "This is Eve."

Yes.

I know them.

I've seen them.

"Come in," Mrs. Wainwright said uncertainly.

The couple sank into the sofa. Eve sat in an armchair.

"I — I don't mean to upset you," Eve began. "I don't even know for sure why I'm here. I live in Fayette — "

"Fayette?" Mrs. Wainwright said. "You traveled all that way alone?"

"How old are you, Eve?" asked Mr. Wainwright.

No. I can't let this distract us.

"Almost seventeen," Eve lied.

The Wainwrights didn't flinch.

"I had to come," Eve barreled on, "because I saw a photo of your daughter, and she looked so much like me." She smiled weakly. "So I guess, what I want to know is . . ."

The words were knotted in her throat.

A tear fell softly down Mrs. Wainwright's cheek.

Mr. Wainwright was looking at her expectantly.

Say it!

"I was adopted," Eve said. "I'm looking for my birth parents."

"Oh, my . . ." Mrs. Wainwright seemed to be

receding into the sofa. Her husband shot her
a look.

That's it.

I was right.

"So . . . I guess that means — " Eve closed
her eyes and took a deep breath. "You're the
ones, right?"

"The ones?" Mr. Wainwright repeated.

"I mean, it's okay and all," Eve added. "I
don't, like, *hate* you or anything. I don't want
you to take me in or give me money or whatever. I guess I just wanted to know who you
were. To see you. And also to ask about
Alexis. To find out how she — "

"Eve," Mr. Wainwright interjected. "We're
not your birth parents. Although I can understand how you might think so."

"You're not?"

Mrs. Wainwright shook her head. "Alexis
was adopted, too."

No.

"But the resemblance — between her and
me — "

"Uncanny," Mr. Wainwright said.

He glanced at his wife uncomfortably.

"Eve," Mrs. Wainwright said, "I'd be willing to bet your parents used the same agency we did — A Better Chance?"

"Yes . . ." Eve replied.

"So perhaps you and Alexis were . . ." Mr. Wainwright began.

Of course.

Sisters, yes. Just not Wainwright *sisters. Not originally.*

"From the same birth mother," Eve said. "Is that what happened? *She gave us both away?*"

"That'd be my guess," Mr. Wainwright said.

Eve felt her eyes welling up.

Now what?

A dead sister. No parents. A train ride for nothing.

Mrs. Wainwright stood up. She knelt next to Eve and put her arms around her. "Eve, it's not a waste. Have dinner with us. Stay overnight. You're tired. We'll tell you everything you want to know about Alexis. We'll even check the adoption records if you like, get A Better Chance's phone number. Nowadays some of the agencies are freer with information."

"I'll prepare the meal," Mr. Wainwright volunteered. "You two can look around the house."

As he went to the kitchen, Eve followed his wife into the basement.

A small corner room was set up as an office. From the back of a metal file cabinet Mrs. Wainwright drew out a folder full of yellowing papers. She began sifting through them. "When Alexis died, I threw out a lot of things. Reminders. But I still have — ah, here it is."

Eve could see the A Better Chance letterhead on the sheet. Mrs. Wainwright picked up her desk phone and tapped out the number. She pressed the SPEAKERPHONE button so Eve could hear.

"Hello?" said a gruff voice.

"Is this A Better Chance?" Mrs. Wainwright asked.

"*Who?*"

"A Better Chance? The adoption agency?"

"Never heard of them."

Click.

"Don't worry." Mrs. Wainwright was reaching for the Yellow Pages now. "There is some sort of central bureau, someplace with a list of all the accredited agencies. . . . *Voilà!*"

She tapped out another number. Put on the speaker. Beeped through several minutes of voice mail.

Finally, a human.

Mrs. Wainwright asked her questions and was put on hold.

Eve felt fluttery as they waited. She nearly jumped when the voice crackled back on the line.

"Hello? The name was A Better Chance?"

Mrs. Wainwright smiled. "Yes. You found them?"

"Uh, not exactly. We have no record of that agency."

"Which means it moved?" Eve asked.

"Which means," the voice replied, "it never existed."

California. Ohio.

Auckland. Bombay.

Cases?

Deaths.

Over one hundred fifty.

And she still doesn't have a clue.

8

"Sorry, ma'am," said another voice over the phone.

By now Eve was used to it.

"Thanks anyway." Eve hung up and turned toward the Wainwrights. "The St. Louis Chamber of Commerce hasn't heard of them, either."

Nor had the hospital there. Or the Better Business Bureau. Or a half dozen other places Eve had called.

Mr. Wainwright was pacing. "Why would someone pull a stunt like this?"

Stolen babies.

Black market.

Kidnappings.

Fly-by-night agencies.

Eve had heard stories. But she'd always put them out of her mind.

Until now.

"I'm sorry." Eve's words sounded so feeble.

"Let's not panic." Mrs. Wainwright began riffling through her papers again. "Who was that doctor we were in contact with?"

"I don't remember," her husband said. "It was a short name. He said he would keep in touch. And he did, for a while. But then he just stopped showing up."

"Look at this." Mrs. Wainwright was slapping papers onto the desk. "I can read our signatures — but not *his.*"

Eve looked at the scribbled, illegible name next to the Wainwrights'. Dr. *Something.*

"His name isn't *printed* anywhere," Mr. Wainwright said. "How could we have been so careless? So *stupid?*"

Mrs. Wainwright touched his arm. "We wanted a baby so badly. We just signed where he told us to."

The two looked so awkward and guilty. Eve stood up. "Maybe I'd better go home. I'm just causing trouble."

"Please don't," Mr. Wainwright said gently. "You came this far. The least we can do is feed and shelter you."

"You must be feeling grubby from the trip," Mrs. Wainwright added. "There's a shower and fresh towels in the upstairs bathroom."

It wasn't a bad idea.

Eve took her backpack upstairs. To get to the bathroom, she had to walk through a bedroom decorated with a thousand posters — sports teams, rock groups, movies — everything just a few years *off*.

Alexis's room, exactly the way she'd left it. Dusted. Kept up.

The three windows, chin-high.

The abstract-pattern wallpaper in shades of purple and black and blue.

The stained-glass hanging light fixture.

I know this place.

Nahhh. Impossible.

Eve quickly left the room and entered a darkened hallway. Her hand reached out and clicked on a light switch on the wall to her left.

She stopped.

How did I know the switch was there?

She closed her eyes and pushed open the bathroom door. *It's an L-shape, with the shower hidden to the left.*

Opening her eyes, she spotted a long tiled room. At the end, to the left, the edge of the shower curtain stuck out from around a corner.

This. Is. Creepy.

She took a deep breath, tried to block out her thoughts, and prepared for her shower.

But the strange feelings didn't stop. Especially as she listened to the Wainwrights' comments over dinner: "Alexis had an appetite like yours." . . . "She hated broccoli, too." . . . "She always sat in that seat."

"It's weird," Eve finally said. "I feel like I *know* some of this stuff about Alexis. As if we're connected."

"Identical twins who are separated at birth often feel that same way," Mr. Wainwright remarked.

"But they're a year apart," Mrs. Wainwright reminded him. *"Fortunately.* You wouldn't want to be identical to Alexis. Then you'd probably have . . . what she had."

"What happened to her?" Eve asked. "At the end, I mean?"

Both Mr. and Mrs. Wainwright's faces tightened.

Ugh.

Subtle as a locomotive.

"The upset stomach," Mrs. Wainwright said. "Constant. Followed by headaches, weakness . . ."

"Soon we could only feed her farina, liquids — just like my grandmother, before she went," Mr. Wainwright said with a rueful smile. "But she was ninety."

"Were there any warning signs?" Eve asked.

Mrs. Wainwright put a hand on Eve's. "You're worried, aren't you? Don't be. The doctors assured us it was a fluke."

"Alexis had a birthmark. Totally normal. Benign," Mr. Wainwright said. "But it began aching. And soon it started to spread, like a rash. From there on, her body just started to give in."

"It all happened so fast," Mrs. Wainwright added.

Eve's appetite was gone. She suddenly felt icy cold.

Slowly she turned and rolled down her turtleneck collar.

The silence told her everything.

She is my sister.

And I'm dead.

Eve tossed in the strange bed.

Mr. and Mrs. Wainwright had tried to reassure her. They'd told her the birthmark was probably irrelevant. That it probably didn't *cause* the disease.

Probably.

Then why does it hurt?

Eve rubbed the birthmark.

Because you've been touching it so much, that's why. GO TO SLEEP.

Impossible.

Eve sat up. Across the floor, the street lamp cast slatted yellow light through the vertical blinds. Like a prison cell.

Dead end.

What now? What about tomorrow?

Back to ski camp. To life. The same as it was, only different forever.

A lifetime of fear. Of being scared by every twinge. Every tiny pain.

Was *this* why her mom and dad had given her up for adoption?

Damaged goods.

How did they know? And why the phantom agency?

It was so *unfair.*

Eve stood up and paced.

Her backpack peeked at her, striped by the incoming light.

She reached for it and pulled out the papers Kate had helped her pack.

Eve had seen most of them before. Computer printouts. Handwritten notes. Web pages. Lists.

Her eyes caught Alexis's name at the top of one list. The heading read DEAD SO FAR.

Charming, Kate.

She quickly skimmed the other names.

Her eyes froze on one.

Bryann Davis, of Racine Junction.

Bryann.

Sad, delicate Bryann.

One of the names. One of the personalities. I used to become. Like Alexis.

"Oh my god," Eve murmured.

Bryann's date of death was three years ago. One year after Alexis. She was fourteen.

Eve frantically looked for the other names. For Danielle and —

Caroline Pomeranz.

The cool one. The one who shut down when things got bad.

Two years ago. Also fourteen.

They were there. Three of them.

Eve's friends. Long-lost friends.

All dead.

Alexis, Bryann, Caroline.

A chill seized Eve's body.

A. B. C.

Four years ago. Three. Two.

D.

Danielle.

What about Danielle?

If she fit the pattern, she should have died a year ago.

Eve read the list over and over.

No Danielle.

She's alive.

74

Or maybe not.

She tried to conjure her up. The way she used to, when she was a child. She tried to see her as she'd be now, age fifteen.

But nothing came to mind.

Have I lost the power?

Or is Danielle dead, too?

Maybe she was, but Kate and Eve simply hadn't found her.

E.

Eve tried to shut out the thought.

E came next.

E was this year.

E for Eve.

Five girls, each born a year apart. Five little deaths, all in a row.

It was absurd. Preposterous.

But the names.

Alexis was real. You've been connected to her your whole life. What about the others?

Tanya?

She was T. She didn't fit.

Neither did many of the other names.

Simple. Others have it, too. Not just you and —

Stop it!

Your sisters.

NO!

Your fourteen-year-old sisters.

Fourteen . . .

She tried to remember what day it was.

She rummaged in her backpack for a calendar and pulled it out.

As she opened it, the sun peeked through the window.

Nine more days.

If she's lucky.

9

"Can't say as I know the name," said the cabdriver. "Racine Junction is a big place."

"Bryann was fourteen," Eve said. "I think she probably looked like me."

"I can drop you off at the junior high school. They might be able to tell you something."

"They're not on vacation?"

"Starts next week."

What luck.

Eve took off her down coat and sat back. Gray industrial buildings whizzed by outside the cab window. Rubble-strewn lots baking in the southern sun. Small attached houses, with young children riding trikes across postage-stamp lawns. So different from Cold Harbor.

Saying good-bye to the Wainwrights that morning had been tough. She could see through their stoic, best-of-luck expressions. She could tell that they didn't want her to leave.

Eve had tried to refuse the money the Wainwrights had offered. But they had insisted. It was enough for plane fare and a week's lodging. *Find your roots*, they'd said. *Bryann's family may not have been as stupid as we were. They may know more.*

Before she left, Eve had called every Davis in the Racine Junction area. No luck. But there were a few unlisted numbers. So she booked a room at the local Y and reserved a seat on the next flight south.

The cab wound through the streets until it arrived at a long tan-brick school building next to a football field.

"Looks like you made it just in time," the driver said.

Kids were beginning to stream from the

80

doors, books slung over shoulders, faces happy. End of school day.

Eve paid her fare and stepped out.

As the cab drove away, she approached the building. Slowly. Trying to make eye contact. Steeling herself for the reactions. For the freaking out.

But it didn't happen.

Nothing.

No recognition.

Now a guy and a girl veered in her direction. Arm in arm. Deep in conversation.

"Um, excuse me?" Eve said. "Do you — *did* you — know Bryann Davis?"

Shrug. Head shake. Nope.

Eve walked onto the school yard. She stopped another couple.

"Never heard of her."

A friendly, eager-looking girl.

"Not in this school."

Eve slumped against the fence. She took off her backpack and pulled out her notes.

Must be a mistake. A typo.

Just great. I'm stuck in the middle of the U.S., looking for someone who doesn't exist.

"You shouldn't be here," a voice said.

A girl. Standing on the other side of the fence.

"Why?" Eve asked.

The girl stared at her, neither nodding nor shaking her head. "You should check the high school. It's down Porterfield Avenue, then left on Brookside."

Duh.

Of course. If Bryann were alive, she'd be seventeen.

"Thanks." Eve took off at a run.

She reached the back of the building first. Through the windows she saw empty class-rooms. She picked up the pace, running along the side of the school, puffing hard under the weight of the pack and her coat. She zoomed around the corner.

Thud.

Contact.

She stumbled backward.

"Watch it!" The guy was stringy-haired, tough-looking, sneering.

"Sorry," Eve exclaimed. "Are you okay?"

The guy's face slackened. "What the — ?"

Yes.

"I'm not who you think I am!" Eve blurted out. "But we might be — someone told me — did you know her?"

The guy began backing away. "Stay there," he said softly. "Just . . . stay there."

She heard his sneakered footsteps slap against the pavement.

Moments later someone else was running back.

Short reddish-brown hair. Freckled. Taller.

Jerry.

Timmy.

Something like that.

He was emerging from the back of her mind. Running toward her, just like this.

Only he was younger, much younger.

And she was —

Bryann.

"Oh . . . my . . . god," she said.

WHERE IS THIS COMING FROM?

He fixed Eve with a hard stare. "Who are you?"

Eve tried to control the shakiness of her voice. "Eve Hardy. Who are you?"

"Terry Bradfield."

Terry. Yes.

"You look familiar. Have you ever lived in Fayette?"

Terry shook his head.

"I do," Eve said. "But I'm — I need to find out about someone. A girl named Bryann — "

Before she could finish, Terry's hand was clutching hers. They were running. Over the field, past an adjacent pond.

"Where are we going?" Eve pleaded.

Terry didn't answer. But when he let go, she followed.

You can trust him.

Eve knew this. Deeply. Somehow.

The street soon became a dirt road, which wound through a wooded area. They stopped at a large clearing.

Eve caught her breath. Nestled into the area was a small village of mobile homes.

Terry led her through the settlement, to a well-kept home decorated with flowers and plotted plants.

"She's working," he said, opening the front door.

"Who?" Eve asked.

"Mrs. Davis. So we don't have to worry. She

won't see you." He stepped inside and gestured for her to come in. "Sit down and make yourself comfortable. I'll be right back."

Comfortable?

Eve stood in the tiny living room. On the opposite wall, surrounded by a gilt-edged, wooden frame, was a poster-sized portrait.

Bryann.

The hair was longer than Eve's, plainer. Her expression was serious, almost gloomy.

But the face was the same.

Eve's face.

Again.

She sat in an armchair, numb.

She couldn't doubt it now.

Sisters.

She, Alexis, and Bryann could have passed for triplets.

In a moment Terry was walking into the room, carrying a cardboard box. He set it down on the carpet and started pulling out papers and notebooks. "All Bryann's stuff," he explained. "We were like brother and sister. We've known each other since we were babies, practically . . ."

Eve watched the pile on the floor grow.

Snapshots. Dance programs. Scribbled notes. Exams and quizzes, almost all marked with A's and A+'s.

Terry was holding a legal pad now. Most of the pages had been written on and folded back. He began unfolding, scanning the pages one by one.

"What's that?" Eve asked.

"Notes for a science report she never had a chance to finish," Terry replied. "Bryann was obsessed with genetics."

"Makes sense," Eve said softly.

Terry looked up with questioning eyes.

"She was adopted, wasn't she?" Eve asked.

"Yes."

"And she liked genetics because she thought it might help her figure out who her birth parents were."

"Well, not exactly."

Eve nodded. "Something about a disease? Did she know about that? Did she think she would get it?"

"Well, yeah. But there was one other thing, too." He held out the legal pad.

Eve took it and read a handwritten title at the top of the page.

Cloning Human Beings

"She thought there were *clones*?" Eve said. "That hasn't ever happened."

"How do you know?" Terry asked. "*Has* it?"

"Bryann was convinced. I never believed it. I used to tease her when she said she had this hunch — about herself. I should have taken her seriously, Eve. Because you . . . and she . . ."

"You mean — ?"

Terry nodded. "And you're a couple of years too late."

She understands.

At last.

New report just in.

Hold it. For now.   —

10

Dear Mom and Dad,
  I guess by now you've tried to reach me once or twice. Kate has told you I was away. Well, she was right, sort of. Actually, I'm farther away than you think. This will sound weird to you, but I need to find out some things about myself.

Eve dropped her pencil and stared out the train window.

I am Bryann.
I am Alexis.

They are Eve.

Not sisters.

Closer.

Closer than identical twins.

Identical *people*.

But how?

Animals were cloned. Plants. Not *humans*. It was illegal.

It was impossible.

Wasn't it?

Of course not. Someone was bound to do it sometime.

That was what Bryann's report had said. The technology existed. It was only a matter of time. Maybe it had happened already.

She knew.

She told Terry.

He didn't believe her at first. I proved it.

What does this mean?

WHAT AM I?

Nobody. Not a real person.

An idea. A theory brought to life. A *thing* in a test tube.

Eve's heart began to flutter.

Fast.

Too fast.

Her chest was on fire.

Every joint in her body cried out in sympathy. With excruciating pain.

It can't be.

The disease. It took Tanya. It took dozens of others on that list — strangers, guys *and* girls — almost exactly the same age.

But it wasn't only strangers. It also killed a girl named Alexis, who happened to be *genetically identical* to Bryann. And Caroline. And Danielle.

And me.

NO!

I AM NOT DYING.

Eve's wrists twinged with a sharp pain. She looked down.

The letter to her parents was balled up in her right fist.

Sleep.

I need sleep. That's all.

Her eyes grew heavy. She leaned back.

By the time her head hit the pillow, she was in a sudden, deep slumber.

She awoke as the train was pulling into North Champlain.

The sun was just peeking over the rail yard. It was colder here, more industrial. Far to the north was the skyline of St. Louis, barely visible over the sprawl of brick buildings.

As she stood, her knees throbbed. Her elbow ached.

Like an old person's.

Stop.

Her footsteps clattered loudly on the tiles of the empty waiting room. At a phone bank, Eve called information and asked for Pomeranz.

No record of the name. Not in North Champlain, not in the surrounding counties.

Eve slammed down the receiver.

Too fast.

Everything was happening too fast.

She hadn't prepared.

At Racine Junction, she and Terry had rushed to the station. They'd made the north train with no time to spare. They should have waited. Done some advance research together. Sure, Terry had promised to do some while she was traveling. . . .

Terry. Of course.

She tapped out his number.

"Yeah?" was the groggy greeting.

"Sorry I woke you up," Eve said. "But it's kind of an emergency — "

"Eve? Where are you?"

"North Champlain. It's morning, Terry. I was on the train all night!"

"Oh. Right. Hey, I'm glad you called, because — "

"Listen, I can't find Caroline Pomeranz's phone number or address. Her family is unlisted."

"They're not unlisted, Eve," Terry said. "After you left, I called North Champlain directory assistance. When the operator came up with nothing, I had her connect me to the police. They knew the Pomeranzes."

"Knew?"

"The parents moved after their daughter died. To Switzerland."

Eve slumped against the side of the phone cubicle.

What a waste. An entire night scrunched up on a train seat, twisting and turning, dreaming about test tubes and mad scientists and rows upon rows of identical Eves, each one fading and dying, like some strange tragic ballet — only to find out, oops, it was all unnecessary, back to square one, dead girls and no clues.

"Now what?" Eve grumbled.

"Switzerland's nice this time of year," Terry said weakly.

"My friend Kate'll love that. 'Hi, Mr. and Mrs. Hardy, Eve's taking another shower and can't come to the phone' — *while I'm halfway around the world looking for the Pomeranzes at a yodeling contest.*"

"Look, you can't give up. Find out about Caroline. From the people who knew her. The way you found out about Bryann. Okay?"

"Do you think it's that simple? Do you think I *like* being all alone in some dumb town in the middle of nowhere?" Eve took a breath. She was shouting. Not good. She lowered her voice. "Sorry, Terry. I'm just tired. Thanks. Really. For everything."

"Anytime. You'll find what you need. Good luck. And call me."

As Eve hung up, she felt a twinge of sadness.

Bryann had good taste.

People were beginning to stream into the station now. Eve had to rest her knees. She sat on a nearby bench, feeling lost and drained.

Her neck was throbbing again. She reached

back and massaged it, but that made it worse.

Leave it alone. And don't jump to conclusions. Of course everything hurts. You were folded up in a plastic seat for ten hours.

Her stomach grumbled. That was a problem, too.

Food would make everything clearer.

Eve straggled out of the station. A wide street, patched and buckling, led straight up a small hill between two rows of warehouses. At the top was a neon sign that spelled out EAT.

Eve climbed the hill. Under the sign she entered an old diner. Tile floors. Formica tables along a plate-glass window. A few groups of older men in flannel shirts, slowly and silently eating their eggs as if they'd been there for years and had ceased to notice each other.

"Seat yourself," a waitress called out.

Sitting at a small table by the window, Eve gazed outside. Down the other side of the hill was a small Main Street — post office, town hall, library, shops.

All vaguely familiar.

Yeah, like any other small town in any TV show.

She glanced at her menu. It was coated with

heavy, yellowing plastic. Graffiti decorated the margins.

Kids.

This place was a hangout. Maybe Caroline used to come here.

"Are you ready?"

The waitress was poised impatiently at Eve's table with pad and pencil.

"Scrambled eggs," Eve began. "Fries, orange juice . . ." *Ask.* "Um, and do you happen to know Caroline Pomeranz?"

"She an actress or something?" the waitress replied without looking up.

"A kid. She used to live here."

"Sweetheart, I know them all. But don't ask me names and faces. I'll get your eggs."

Useless.

As Eve put back the menu, she looked at the graffiti — JW & RT, EAT GRILLED CHEESE & DIE, HI BETH! JUNIOR CLASS RULES!!!

She smiled.

Just like the Fayette Junior High School yearbook.

The thought of home gnawed at her. She missed it. And school, sort of. Well, at least the yearbook meetings. The book was going to be great this year.

If I ever see it.

Eve gazed out onto the street. At the commuters vying for parking spots. The morning dog walkers. The plaid-skirted woman opening the tomblike stone library.

Library.

Yearbook.

Eve slid out of her seat. Her back twinged angrily as she stood up and headed for the door.

"Hey! What about your eggs?" shouted the waitress.

"You have them!" Eve replied.

She pulled some money out of her pocket, slapped it on the table, and left.

The librarian looked up from her desk as Eve walked in. "Do my eyes deceive me? A high school kid *here* on a vacation morning?"

Eve smiled. "Junior high. Do you have copies of the school yearbooks?"

The librarian pointed the way. Eve found the section — a row of yearbooks, *decades'* worth. She took down the one from two years ago and began flipping through the graduating-class photos.

P . . .

Palladino . . . Peterson . . . Pinsky . . .

Caroline Pomeranz.

There.

Caroline had still been alive by the deadline for yearbook entries.

Her skin was pale, her hair short and black and cut at a weird angle. Lots of earrings and a stud on the left side of her nose. Crossed arms over a black shirt, revealing long, black fingernails.

Gothic. That makes sense.

The imaginary Caroline had been *different.* Her own person. She hadn't cared what her parents thought, even at age six.

Under Caroline's school picture was a group of smaller photos. Caroline at a club, dancing. Leaning against a tree, scowling. Arms around the shoulders of another girl.

Under that last photo was the printed message HP & CP BFF!

BFF. Best Friends Forever.

Perfect.

Who was HP?

Eve stared at the girl's face. *Yes. I know her.*

Polly . . . no, H. Holly. She went back to the beginning of the P's and checked photo by photo until she found the same likeness.

Holly Petrou.

She shivered.

When she looked up, she noticed the librarian watching her. Curious. Concerned.

"Do you have a pay phone?" Eve blurted out.

"Near the entrance," the librarian answered.

Eve tried to run, but her legs nearly gave out.

Slow down.

Local directory assistance. One Petrou. Listed.

Eve was shaking as she called the number.

"Hello?" said a young voice.

"May I speak to Holly?" Eve asked.

Silence.

Then, quietly, "This is Holly. Who's this?"

"Well, you don't know me, but — "

"I don't believe this. Of course I know you."

"You *do*?"

"The . . ." Holly lowered her voice to a whisper. "The clone, right?"

"How did you — ?"

"It's Caroline's voice — who else could it be? Where are you?"

101

"At the library. But — "

"I'll be right there."

Click.

Eve stared at the receiver for a moment, then hung up.

She knows. Everything.

Impossible.

Dazed, she wandered back into the reading room.

"Are you okay?" the librarian asked.

"Fine," Eve mumbled.

Just a clone about to meet a total stranger who seems to already know me. Plus, my body aches and my heart's weak and I don't have long to live. But otherwise things are swell.

Eve had barely put away the yearbook when a heavyset, grinning girl came racing into the library.

Pale face, black clothing. Everything Gothic. Just like Caroline.

"Look at you," Holly said. "You are so . . . *straight*. But that's cool. I am *so* glad you came. Where have you been?"

Yes. The voice. The face. The mannerisms.

It was all familiar. *Why?*

"Been? Uh, home. Holly, I don't know how you could — "

"Did you find Dr. Black?"

"I mean, have we ever — ?"

Eve swallowed the rest of the question.

It was a short name. That's what Mr. Wainwright had said. About the doctor from A Better Chance.

"Who's Dr. Black?" Eve demanded.

Holly's smile faded. "You told *me* about him. Remember? Over the phone? The clone guy. You and Caroline tried looking him up, but there were about a million Dr. Blacks listed in the physician directory — "

"Holly, I never called you. I've never known about you until right this moment!"

"Wait a minute. What's your name?"

"Eve!"

"You're *not* the girl . . ."

"No! Who did you *think* I was?"

Holly's mascara and eyeliner seemed to darken as her face grew ashen. "Her name was Danielle."

A boy in Kansas City. Lou Gehrig's disease.

Female, Manitoba. Rheumatoid arthritis.

Massive stroke. Male, Guatemala.

Alive?

All, so far.

Their lives, I'm afraid, are in
the hands of the Fayette girl.

11

"**W**hat city, please?" squawked the mechanical voice.

Eve massaged her aching forehead. She focused on Holly across the bedroom. "Uh . . . Huddlestone — ?"

Holly looked up from her desk chair. "Huddles*ton*," she corrected. "Huddleston Falls."

Eve repeated it. Softly.

If she kept her head still, it didn't hurt.

"Name, please?" the voice asked.

"Forbes."

Danielle Forbes of Huddleston Falls. That

was all Holly could find out. The information was scribbled in one of Caroline's English notebooks.

Holly had tried to piece together the phone conversation. Danielle had sounded desperate. She'd known about the cloning and the disease. And she had been determined not to get what Caroline had gotten.

Holly didn't know what had happened to Danielle. She just stopped calling. Never left a return phone number.

But she'd gotten further than I have. She knew about Dr. Black.

And maybe more. Maybe she'd met him. Maybe she'd figured out how to beat the disease.

Maybe she was still alive.

Danielle was Eve's only hope.

"The number is . . . 555-9126," said the recorded voice.

Eve scribbled it down and quickly called.

Holly paced her bedroom floor. "I can't stand this."

At the other end, a *click*. A pickup. "Hello, you've reached the Forbes family. No one can come to the phone right now. . . ."

It was scratchy. A bad connection.

The static hurt.

But the voice seemed familiar.

Like mine.

"What?" Holly was gaping at her. *"Why are you looking like that, Eve?"*

" . . . Please leave a message at the sound of the tone."

"I think — it sounds like — " Eve stammered, hand over the receiver. *She's alive.*

Beeeeeep.

"Hello?" Eve said into the phone. "This is Eve. I'm . . . what Caroline was, only a year younger — than *Danielle*, not Caroline — I'm two years younger than her, or *you*, but I need to find Dr. Black; I think I'm getting what you had, and — whenever the next train to Huddleston Falls is, from North Champlain, that's the one I'm taking. I'll call you from there, okay? Sorry about this. But I'm kind of in a hurry. See you."

She hung up the phone and groaned. "She's not going to understand one word of that."

Holly was putting her coat back on. "I did. You were brilliant. Now let's get out of here."

* * *

Six hours.

Each bump was a wrenching jolt.

The clacking of the tracks seemed to be taunting her: *Dead-dead. Dead-dead. Dead-dead.*

Sleep was out of the question. The pain wouldn't ease up.

Neither would the worry.

But it'll be gone soon. Danielle survived. She knows how to beat this.

Eve decided to rewrite the letter she had started — slowly, parceling out the words a few at a time, as long as her aching fingers could stand it. She told her parents *everything*. Where she had been, where she was headed. By the time they got it, she'd be heading home.

She hoped.

Love, Eve she wrote, and then carefully inserted the letter into an envelope and sealed it.

As the train pulled into Huddleston Falls, Eve pressed her nose to the window. Darkness had swallowed up the suburban countryside, leaving a cozy tapestry of lights. The station was a fluorescent beacon in the midst of town. Several weary commuters stood at the platform, catching the end of evening rush hour.

No clone in sight.

Stepping off the train, Eve clutched the metal railing. Her ankles were screaming at her. She gazed up and down, watching people walk briskly to waiting cars. She dropped her letter into a mailbox near the newspaper vending machines.

And then she saw her.

A girl, wrapped in a thick, hooded down parka, emerging from a station door farther down the platform. She was gazing in the opposite direction. Eve couldn't make out her features in the shadow of the hood, but the height was exactly Eve's.

"Danielle?" she called out.

The girl spun around. "Eve?"

Eve hobbled toward her, gritting her teeth with the pain. "I am *so* glad to see you! I saw Holly. She told me all about — "

She stopped.

Blue eyes.

Blond hair.

111

"Oh. Sorry," Eve said. "I thought you were . . ."

"Unbelievable," the girl said, staring at Eve with wonder. "It's as if I'm looking at her."

Eve nodded. "So . . . you must be Danielle's . . ."

"Older sister. Martina."

Eve sat on a bench. She was short of breath. "Well, I guess . . . you know what happened . . . with the clones and all. And Dr. Black."

"Yes, but we had no idea he'd made another one — after Danielle." Smiling, Martina sat next to Eve. "Guess he still had some leftover genes."

"You have no idea how frustrating it's been — well, I guess you do, I mean, Danielle has been through this, but — oh, I am *so* relieved, Martina —my head hurts, my neck is killing me — "

"I'll take you to our house. The car's in the lot."

Martina helped Eve up. Arm in arm, they walked toward the end of the platform.

"I can't wait to meet Danielle," Eve said. "I

think it's so weird to have, like, an identical copy of myself. Alive."

Martina turned. Her smile had vanished.

Eve's heart stopped.

"You thought . . ." Martina's voice trailed off.

"She's not?" Eve asked.

Martina shook her head. "About a year ago."

And Eve suddenly realized whose voice she'd heard on that answering machine.

Martina's.

Not Danielle's.

WATCHERS
Case File: 0918

Name: Danielle Forbes

Age: 14

First contact: 39:11:27

DECEASED.

12

"Don't . . . make . . . a sound," Martina whispered.

She and Eve tiptoed through the first floor of the Forbes house. A TV laugh track brayed from a room near the stairs.

"Hi!" Martina called out cheerfully.

Two absent-sounding hellos echoed from the den.

Martina gestured frantically for Eve to go up.

The first step was like climbing a fence. Eve's calf muscles felt as if they'd rip. Her ankles wobbled. Her hips were on fire.

"Hurry!" Martina whispered.

"Help me!" Eve whispered back.

Martina took her arm. Eve leaned on her and painfully stepped upward.

"This happened to Danielle, too," Martina said. "Some kind of clone disease, huh?"

"It's happening to other kids across the country. Not just us clones."

Eve grimaced. She wasn't sure what hurt more, the physical pain or the despair.

She's dead. She had my symptoms. She never found Dr. Black.

She was my last lead.

But Martina had insisted they come home. Look at Danielle's stuff. Try to continue the search.

Martina had hope. Which was a good thing.

She would have to have enough for two.

Eve was exhausted when she reached the top of the stairs. "I . . . have to lie down," she said.

Straight ahead was an open door into what must have been Martina's bedroom. It looked neat but lived-in.

Martina was quietly opening a door to the left, flicking on a light switch.

The room was empty of furniture. Musty-smelling. Its wood-plank floor was covered with a thin coat of dust.

"This was Danielle's room." Martina's whisper echoed faintly against the bare walls as she closed the door behind them and walked toward a closet. "Mom and Dad wanted to get rid of all visual reminders. They're still so torn up. Which is why they mustn't see you. Anyway, they stored some of Danielle's stuff in here, the sentimental things they couldn't bear to throw out. They would kill me if they knew I was doing this."

"Don't they know about the clones?"

Martina pulled open the the closet door. She began rummaging around a pile of cardboard boxes inside. "Danielle managed to track Caroline down, not long before the end. She told Mom and Dad, and they were pretty freaked out."

"How about Bryann and Alexis?"

"Who?"

"The other clones. Did Danielle know about them, too?"

Martina was carrying out a box now, setting it on the floor. "No. But she suspected there were others. Here — *this* is what I was looking for."

She pushed aside an old bike chain. Under it was a small, battered spiral notebook. She began flipping through it. "Danielle had this with her on the bus when she died."

"She died on a *bus*?"

Martina nodded. "She was looking for Dr. Black. By that time she was really sick. Mom and Dad wouldn't allow her to go, so she snuck out."

She held out the notebook, open. Eve took it and read:

April 9

Mom and Dad never trusted Dr. Black, right from the beginning. He never gave his first name. He answered his own phone. No assistants. They are SO paranoid to begin with, and they figured I'd been kidnapped from some unsuspecting mother or something. They couldn't just take me, pay the money, and go.

They did some snooping around. Knowing Dad, he probably hired a detective or something. Anyway, they saved this:

April 13
Just back from libe. Found an article
about Dr. Horatio Black:

HUMAN CLONES IN OUR LIFETIME

St. Louis — Within the next few decades, even sooner, we may be shaking hands with ourselves on the street. Or raising children in our exact likeness, but without any of our flaws. These are the tantalizing visions outlined by Dr. Horatio P. Black, geneticist affiliated with Trueman Bell Hospital.

In a conference today, Dr. Black was quick to point out that these sci-fi scenarios are not the primary reason for the exploration of cloning techniques. "Clones would have immense lifesaving potential. Imagine, for example, that you have bone marrow cancer. A matching donor is extremely difficult to find. So we take a sample of your genetic material, manipulate the code, and then produce your clone — identical to you in all ways, except for healthy bone marrow. That clone could donate marrow, and your body would have zero chance of rejection."

Dr. Black paused before the rapt crowd. When he spoke again, his voice was subdued: "If I had been able to produce a clone, I may have been able to save my daughter." Dr. Black's daughter, Laura, died three years ago under circumstances he did not specify.

April 16

Tomorrow I take the bus to St. Louis. I feel TERRIBLE not telling Mom and Dad, but I CAN'T. They would never say yes to a trip like this.

"She never made it, huh?" Eve said.

Martina shook her head. "Mom and Dad are still devastated. And angry. And hurt. They couldn't be with her. They couldn't help. She died all alone. And in such pain."

A sharp twinge shot through Eve.

And this is what she felt like. A body falling apart.

"You have to find him," Martina said. "You don't have much time —"

122

She stopped abruptly, cut off by the sound of thumping footsteps.

Heading up the stairs.

"Martina?" Mr. Forbes's voice. "What do you think you're doing?"

Four more. Today.

Deceased.

Two in North America —

Please. Later.

13

"Go!" Martina pushed.

Eve dived.

She landed on the closet floor with a soft thud. Martina shut the door behind her.

Pain.

Knifelike, searing pain. As if her brain had been smashed out of her ears.

Don't scream.

Bite. Tongue.

Voices. Angry. Outside the door, arguing.

A metallic clank.

". . . only a bike chain . . ." Martina's words

were becoming clear. "I need it, and Danielle would have wanted me to — "

"That's not the point," her dad interrupted. "These things are all we have of your sister. We've *asked* you to leave them alone until *we* could sort them out."

"Sorry, Dad."

"Now, clean up and come downstairs. And next time you need something, ask us first."

Eve heard the bedroom door close. Footsteps down the stairs.

Then, silence.

The closet door opened. Martina poked her head in. "Are you okay?"

"I've been better."

"Anyway, you see why they can't meet you? They're still so attached. They would have heart attacks if they — "

"Martina," Eve interrupted, "we . . . have to . . . hurry."

Martina felt her forehead. "You're feverish."

"Jumping in the closet — I thought I broke my hip."

"That's not good."

"I know it's not. What am I going to do?"

128

"*We*," Martina replied. "I'm with you, Eve. Just hang in there. Mom and Dad'll be going to bed after the news. That's about ten minutes. We'll wait for them to fall asleep. Another twenty minutes."

"Then what?"

"I don't know. But I'll think of something. Just sit back and rest. And don't worry."

With that, she shut the door.

Eeeeeee . . . eeeeeee . . .

The stairway floorboards creaked beneath their feet.

As they reached bottom and tiptoed through the kitchen, Eve glanced at the stove clock.

12:07 A.M.

Martina pulled open the door of the attached garage.

"Are you sure this is all right?" Eve whispered.

"I've been to St. Louis a million times," Martina replied, unlocking the family car doors.

"*Your parents* — aren't they going to kill you for doing this?"

Martina gently helped Eve into the passenger seat. "Eve, I didn't believe my sister when she told me about the clones. That's why she snuck off alone — because no one took her seriously. I'm not going to let that happen again."

Martina climbed into the car and backed it into the street. Then she took off, steering her way through the darkened town.

Within moments they were speeding along the freeway. Eve gazed listlessly out the window at the sleepy neighboring villages. The slanted roofs seemed to dance by, frosted by the light of the full moon. An occasional glowing window winked at her.

People still up. Watching a movie. Reading. Worrying.

She would change places with any of them in a minute.

"Why would he do it, Martina?" Eve asked. "Why the phony adoption agency?"

Martina shrugged. "To keep the clones a secret, I guess. So no one could trace him. Cloning is controversial. People think it's *wrong*. Like messing with nature."

"But if he's afraid of being discovered, then

why *four* of us? Why not stop at one?"

"Why don't people stop at one atom bomb? Or one thousand? Once they make it, they have to do it again and again. Improving it."

"How did he improve us? We're all defective. We all die."

Martina sighed. "Danielle thought he gave the gene to all of you. On purpose."

"Why?"

"To observe you, then get you out of the way before you were old enough to figure out what happened. Sick, isn't it?"

No. Not sick.

Worse than that.

Murder.

Eve gazed grimly back out the window.

That's what I am — not just a scientific curiosity.

Worse than that. Worse than a nonperson.

A death experiment.

The wintry silence was broken only by the engine's hum as Martina exited the freeway. She steered grimly through the outskirts of St. Louis, reading off the street signs.

Eve navigated the way to Laramie Drive, a long boulevard of commercial buildings.

"Slow down," Eve said, reading off Danielle's journal. "We need number one-seven-four-nine."

Martina slowed down. "Sixteen ninety-seven . . ." she read.

Eve squinted.

1727 was a Laundromat.

1731, a flower shop.

Then a huge parking lot.

The next building was the Trueman Bell Hospital.

Number 1765.

"We missed it!" Eve blurted out.

Martina slammed on the brakes. "I didn't see it."

"Neither did I."

Martina circled around the block and slowly passed the buildings again. She glided to a stop in front of the parking lot. "It should be here. Between thirty-one and sixty-five!"

Eve stared at a sign that stretched over the entrance gate:

PUBLIC PARKING
BRAND-NEW, SECURE FACILITY
REASONABLE RATES

"It must have been here," Eve remarked. "They tore it down. For parking."

"Okay. Okay. Don't panic," Martina said. "They didn't tear down Dr. Black *with* it. We can ask at the hospital. Someone will know what happened."

She pulled to a stop at the curb, climbed out, and began running toward the hospital entrance.

Eve squeezed the door handle. Her hands felt as if they'd burst into flames. *"Martina!"*

The door flew open. Eve swung her hips, but her legs stayed in the car.

She fell, missing the curb only because Martina caught her.

"My joints . . ." Eve said through gritted teeth.

"Hang on," Martina urged, lifting Eve to her feet. "It's not far."

Arthritis.

Eve thought of her grandmother. The way she used to totter around before she was shut up in the nursing home. The way she always complained about the pain.

This shouldn't be happening to me!

Arm in arm, she and Martina walked up

the ramp, through the sliding doors, and into the front lobby.

A man eyed them curiously from behind a reception desk.

"Dr. Black, please," Martina called out.

The man punched the name into a computer and shook his head. "No one by that name here."

"He used to be at the address next door," Eve insisted.

"Well, he's not here now," the man replied.

"Well, give us somebody who would know him," Martina snapped.

The man shot her a dirty look, then spoke into an intercom: "Paging Dr. Rudin. Front desk."

Eve's ankle gave out. She grabbed Martina, nearly pulling her to the floor. "Owwwww . . ."

Cold. Hot. Freezing. HOT.

Eve's body was short-circuiting. She pointed frantically to the seats near the wall.

By the time Martina settled her in, a crisply dressed, youngish woman with dark hair and glasses was walking toward them. "I'm Dr. Rudin, the night administrator. Can I help you?"

"Dr. Black!" Eve's throat was burning now. The words hurt.

"Excuse me?" Dr. Rudin said.

"We know his old address — seventeen forty-nine — but the building's not there," Martina explained. "The guy behind the desk said you'd know him."

"*Who?*"

"Dr. Black!"

"Dr. Black is no longer with us. But if you'll tell me what's wrong, I can direct you to any number of specialists — "

"*You don't understand!*" Martina said. "Look. I have a car. You tell me where Dr. Black is, and we're there. If he's in Bermuda, we're on the next plane. *Just tell us.*"

Dr. Rudin put her hand gently on Martina's shoulder. "What I'm trying to say is, you *can't* see him. No one can."

Eve knew what was coming next. It was a pattern.

Don't say it.

Just don't.

"Dr. Black," the administrator went on, "passed away about six years ago."

Her.

Rudin.

The file is linked.

She was there. At the beginning.

Does the girl remember?

How could she?

14

*D*ead.

Alexis, Bryann, Caroline, Danielle. And now Dr. Black.

"Did you know him?" Martina asked.

Dr. Rudin nodded. "No one did, really. I worked with him when I was just starting out, as an intern."

The experiment is over.

Well, almost.

Just one more lab rat to go.

Congratulations, Dr. Black.

Eve slumped into her seat.

But Martina was pressing on, asking questions.

". . . He spent most of his time at home," Dr. Rudin was saying, "especially after the death of his two daughters. He had a lab there, and he loved doing research."

Two daughters?

Eve thought back to Danielle's news clippings.

There was only one daughter. Laura . . . "died three years ago under circumstances he did not specify."

"What happened to the stuff in his lab?" Martina asked.

Dr. Rudin shrugged. "Thrown out, I imagine. Why do you ask? Are you girls related to him?"

"Well, no, not exactly." Martina shot Eve a look.

It's over.

Go home.

Be with your family. Don't die alone, like Danielle.

"Let's just go, Martina," Eve said.

She suddenly felt a hand on her forehead.

"You're feverish," Dr. Rudin said. "Come with me."

"No," Eve protested. "Dr. Rudin, I — I have something you can't cure."

Dr. Rudin smiled. "I'll be the judge of that."

"It's the telomere thing!" Martina blurted out. "That weird disease, where the body ages? Have you heard of it?"

"Yes," Dr. Rudin said, giving Eve a questioning look. "But there's no reliable diagnosis — "

"Eve was *given* the disease, Dr. Rudin," Martina said. "She's a clone. I know it sounds ridiculous, but there were four of them. Dr. Black created them."

Dr. Rudin narrowed her eyes at Eve. "What did you say your name was?"

"Eve Hardy. Look, I just need to get home — "

"Eve . . ." Dr. Rudin sat. She reached out and swept back Eve's hair, examining the back of her neck.

The birthmark.

"Oh my lord . . ." Dr. Rudin muttered.

"My sister had that mark, too!" Martina said. "Her name was Danielle."

Dr. Rudin nodded. "I . . . I know."

"You *do*?" Martina exclaimed. "How?"

"I was there right after you were born, Eve," Dr. Rudin said softly. "Danielle, too. He said you were both left at the hospital doorstep, anonymously. You must be . . . fourteen."

Eve nodded. *No words. Please. Too much pain.*

"Danielle died at this age," Martina explained. "She was convinced Dr. Black was working on a cure for the disease."

Dr. Rudin quickly took a prescription pad from her jacket pocket, ripped off a sheet, and began writing on the back. "This is the address. Go now. See what you can find. Notes. Anything. Call me when you get there."

Eve felt an arm lift her on the right. Another on the left. She felt herself being walked outside. It was cold.

Cold.

Sleep.

She thought she heard "Good night." But it might have been "Good luck." She wasn't sure.

By the time the back of her head hit the seat, she was unconscious.

"Eve, wake up! We're here!"

Shoulder.

Pain.

Sharp.

Eve's eyes opened.

"The new owners are the Feltons," Martina continued. "Doctor Howard and Doctor Felicia. Both professors. I woke them up. They almost threw me out, but I told them what happened."

Martina began pulling Eve out of the car. Pain radiated fiercely across her back.

The walk to the front door seemed like a mile uphill.

The Doctors Felton were a balding man and a trim gray-haired woman. Standing in the front door in their pj's, they looked at Eve with concern and fear.

"I — I don't know if we can help you," Dr. Howard Felton said. "We turned Doctor Black's lab into a dining room, which was its original function — "

To the left. Wood paneling.

He led them to the left, into a medium-sized room, paneled in oak.

"I . . . know . . . this . . . place," Eve murmured. "It was . . . different."

Glass. Lights. Liquid.

So bright.

So cold.

"There was a lot of equipment here when we came to look at the house," Dr. Felicia Felton said. "Test tubes, beakers, spectrometers, a magnetic resonance imaging machine — "

"Did he leave any notes?" Martina asked. "Did you save anything?"

"No." Dr. Howard Felton shook his head. "It wasn't relevant to our line of work."

Eve's knees gave in. Her head began to spin.

Martina grabbed her by the arm. Dr. Felicia Felton pulled out a dining room chair.

Round and round and round she goes . . .

"EVE!" Martina was shouting.

This is what it's like to die. A slow fade. Not too bad, really.

"Eve, you have to concentrate!"

Focus.

"Is anything familiar, Eve?"

Martina was running. In and out of sight. Pulling up the carpets. Knocking on the walls. Looking behind paintings. The professors were protesting. Telling her how expensive everything was.

The door.

It was right next to the painting of the rowboat.

A brass handle and hinges. Hidden in the paneling.

Speak.

"What's . . . inside?" Eve rasped, nodding toward the door.

"Nothing," said Dr. Felicia Felton. "An old dumbwaiter. Used to deliver food from the kitchen, which was once in the basement. It was broken when we moved in."

Dr. Howard Felton yanked open the door.

Blackness. Two dangling ropes. Like a miniature elevator shaft.

Martina reached in and pulled on a rope. "It's stuck."

"Hasn't been used in decades," Dr. Howard Felton said.

Button.

It was by the corner. It looked like a light switch.

Eve reached toward it. "Press."

"It doesn't work — " Dr. Felicia Felton protested.

But Martina was already there. She pounded the button, once. Twice.

Nothing.

The ropes.

"Pull," Eve said.

"I *did* already."

"Pull."

Martina yanked the ropes again.

Clink.

"Glass," Martina said. "There's something in the dumbwaiter."

The Feltons reached in and helped her.

Rrrrrrrrrrr.

A dull, rubbing sound.

"Easy!" admonished Dr. Felicia Felton. "Don't break anything."

RRRRRRRRR . . .

There.

A small platform was lowering into the opening. The floor of a small, boxlike enclosure. Martina wedged her fingers onto it and pulled down.

The first thing Eve saw was the notebooks.

A fallen pile of them. Scattered about.

Behind them were tubes. Flasks. Diagrams pinned to the rear wall.

Photos.

Two of them. Framed.

One was of a teenage girl, someone Eve had never seen before.

The other was Eve.

She has to find the serum.

*Four more cases reported, in America. Sick
but still alive.*

Two in the same family. In Australia.

She must read the lab reports first.

Sweden. The first report there.

Does she have enough time?

Zaire . . .

Portugal . . .

Pakistan . . .

Well? Does she?

15

"'I'd thought the death of a wife was the worst a man could bear,'" read Martina from a yellowed spiral notebook. "'Now my dear Laura is gone, too, and I find depths of grief I've never known. Whitney is all I have left — and today I discover that she has the gene, too! That she, too, may not reach adolescence. I can barely think. But I must. I have to redouble my efforts at a cure. I believe the defective gene is appearing in other areas of the country.'"

"That was nineteen years ago," Dr. Howard Fenton said, looking over her shoulder.

Fading . . . falling.

Keep. Your. Eyes. Open.

"What . . . cure?" Eve said.

Martina flipped through the book, scanning the pages. " 'Not sure treatments will work. Don't seem to be affecting Whitney. Have made major breakthrough today in replication technique. Am now ready to incubate somatic cell taken from Whitney last week. Perhaps I will be able to correct the defect on a genetic level.' *This is it!* Eve, he cloned his second daughter! That's who you are!"

The photo. Not me. Another daughter. Whitney.

"This is *incredible!*" Martina was skimming like crazy. "Here's Alexis. The first success. He's, like, ecstatic. Here's Bryann. And Caroline. Danielle . . ."

"Go . . . to the end," Eve said.

Martina flipped to the last entry and read: " 'Can't bear it. A life of total, abject failure. Whitney is gone now. The cures were of no use. The clones have the mutation — all of them. Was not able to manipulate their genes

152

at all. Fortunately they do not know. Neither do the parents. Some of them suspect the fake adoption agency, but my talent at deception never fails to amaze me.

" 'I must not give up on the girls. If I do, their deaths are my fault. If I do, I give up on all humanity. Others should not have to go through what I have.

" 'One of the new treatments has worked perfectly in the experimental trials. Had planned to try each treatment on a different girl. Instead I will change the vials. Give them all the same. The new one. Will contact the parents tomorrow.' "

Martina fell silent.

"Yes?" Dr. Felicia Felton asked.

"That's it," Martina said. "The rest of the pages are blank."

Dr. Howard Felton took the book and flipped back a page. "February twenty-one. If I remember correctly, he died that month."

"Where are the new treatments?" Martina was pulling down test tubes, reading labels.

The Feltons reached in, grabbing at whatever they could.

Stand.

Eve struggled to her feet. Holding the edge of the table, she dragged herself closer to the dumbwaiter.

She had her eye on the corner of the enclosure.

On a small cardboard box marked VACUUM CLEANER BAGS.

She put her hand on Martina's shoulder. For support.

"What are you doing?" Martina cried out. "Sit!"

Eve reached in. She pulled out the box and fell backward.

The Feltons caught her and sat her down.

"What? *What?*" Martina ripped open the box. She pulled out decayed newspaper padding.

At the bottom, mixed with shreds of paper, were a few small vials. Each had a dull-colored liquid inside it.

Martina picked up one of the vials and read the label. "Bryann."

"All the treatments are different," Dr. Felicia Felton remarked. "Which is the one that works?"

"He didn't say!" Martina replied.

Eve reached in. She turned other vials and read the labels. CAROLINE. ALEXIS.

EVE.

The one meant for her.

She lifted it out.

"Wait!" Martina cried. "What if it's not the right one?"

Eve paused.

Her mind was clouded.

What if?

The wrong one meant death.

But how to pick?

The clearest one? That was Alexis's.

The strongest looking? Caroline's. It was dark green.

The fullest vial? Bryann's.

No.

The answer worked its way up. It shot through the murk in her brain.

Each vial was meant for one girl. Each a different fate. Assigned by Dr. Black.

Fate.

It was something Eve understood.

It had guided her here.

It would guide her now.

She would not steal anyone else's.

She had to face her own.

Eve looked at Martina. She tried to speak, but even that took too much effort.

Martina was not crying. Her eyes were locked on Eve's.

She knew.

Somehow, she knew.

No.

More.

Time.

She tried twisting off the top of the vial, but her fingers wouldn't grip.

I'm going.

Like Danielle.

Away from home.

Missing in action.

The room was swirling.

The air was leaking from her lungs.

The lights were dimming.

Take it.

A white light formed in the center of the room. Or was it in her brain? Her imagination? She couldn't tell.

In the center of the light were faces. Blurry but slowly assuming familiar shapes.

Alexis.

Bryann.

Caroline.

Danielle.

Eve smiled. "Hey, guys . . ."

"EVE! EEEEEEEVE!"

Martina's voice.

Eve felt something pour into her mouth.

And all went black.

A	Deceased.
B	Deceased.
C	Deceased.
D	Deceased.
E	Pending.

16

*O*ut of the blackness.
Light.
White light.
Objects, too. Blurry. Moving. Hovering.
(Faces.)
Mom.
Dad.
Kate.
Martina. (Why is SHE with them?)
Looking at me. (Mad. They must be.)
I never said good-bye.
SORRY!

(You failed. You should have stayed home.)

"Eve?"

Dr. Rudin.

TELL THEM! TELL THEM WHAT HAP-PENED —

"Eve, wake up!"

Eve's eyes flickered open.

"Yo, is she alive?" *(Kate.)*

"Haaaagerrrfffol . . ." Moving her mouth felt like lifting weights.

Swallow. Cough.

"What'd she say?" *(Martina.)*

"Give her a chance. She's been out a long time." *(Dr. Rudin.)*

Eve blinked.

The room came into focus.

White walls. Fluorescent lights. IV tubes.

She slowly scanned the room.

They were smiling. All of them.

Her parents. Her two friends. Dr. Rudin.

Real.

Alive.

"Eve?" said Mrs. Hardy, taking her hand.

"I — I'm sorry, Mom. I didn't mean to — "

"Shhhh," said her dad. "You did the right thing. Dr. Rudin told us what happened."

"She did? How did you all get here so fast?"

"You've been unconscious for three days," Dr. Rudin replied.

The serum.

"It — worked?" Eve asked.

Dr. Rudin nodded. "I thought we'd lost you at first. But your blood seems to be stabilizing, and the symptoms are slowly going away. I have one team running a check on the telomere activity of your chromosomes — and I've hired a lab to replicate the serum. This is huge, Eve. This will be public news very soon."

"Which means no one else will have to suffer like you did," Martina said.

And Danielle.

And Alexis and Bryann and Caroline.

Whitney, too. The first. The donor.

All a part of Eve.

All gone.

Sacrificed.

For the love of Dr. Black's daughter.

"It was wrong for him to do that," Eve said.

Dr. Rudin touched her hand. "But look what came out of it. A treatment for a new disease, something that no one has understood. Except Dr. Black."

"But the cloning — "

"Perhaps someday we'll find Dr. Black's notes about that, too. So . . . many good consequences, right?"

Eve turned away.

She wasn't so sure.

"Danielle is still alive, Eve," Martina said, "in you."

"So are the others," Kate added.

And they would stay alive. In Eve's brain. Their memories flashing in and out at odd times. Haunting her the rest of her life.

"Guess I'm the end of the line, huh?" Eve said.

"The survivor," her dad replied.

Eve's mind was beginning to drift. "Do me a favor, Dr. Rudin," she said. "If you do find the notes — about the cloning — destroy them."

She didn't hear the answer.

Her eyes were closing. Words from the real world were fading, mingling with dreams.

". . . give her some time . . ." *(Dr. Rudin.)*

". . . so drained . . ." *(Mom.)*

Then, sudden footsteps.

Agitated voices.

"Miss, you can't go in there!"

Wake up.

A new voice.

Urgent. Confused.

Eve's eyes blinked open.

"Eve?"

She turned, slowly, painfully, to the person standing by the bed.

A down coat, a wool scarf.

A face.

No.

Impossible.

"Hi," the girl said. "You don't know me . . ."

A dream.

ABCDE. No one left. I am the end of the line.

". . . but my name is Francesca. . . ."

Marion Ettlinger

ABOUT THE AUTHOR

Peter Lerangis is the author of more than one hundred books, including two Young Adult thrillers, *The Yearbook* and *Driver's Dead*. He was once a stage actor, which often allowed him to travel into the past. He still enjoys doing it as an author, although he misses the costumes. Mr. Lerangis lives in New York City with his wife, Tina deVaron, and his two sons, Nick and Joe.